Thomas Howard

On the Loss of Teeth

Anatiposi

Thomas Howard

On the Loss of Teeth

Reprint of the original.

1st Edition 2023　|　ISBN: 978-3-38230-552-9

Anatiposi Verlag is an imprint of Outlook Verlagsgesellschaft mbH.

Verlag (Publisher): Outlook Verlag GmbH, Zeilweg 44, 60439 Frankfurt, Deutschland
Vertretungsberechtigt (Authorized to represent): E. Roepke, Zeilweg 44, 60439 Frankfurt, Deutschland
Druck (Print): Books on Demand GmbH, In de Tarpen 42, 22848 Norderstedt, Deutschland

ON THE

LOSS OF TEETH;

AND ON THE

BEST MEANS OF RESTORING THEM.

BY

THOMAS HOWARD,

Surgeon Dentist

To His Grace THE ARCHBISHOP OF CANTERBURY,

17, GEORGE STREET, HANOVER SQUARE

LONDON.

~~~~~~~~~~

" Avec de mauvaises dents jamais femme n'étoit belle,
Avec de jolies dents jamais femme n'étoit laide."

J. J. ROUSSEAU.

~~~~~~~~~~

LONDON:
SIMPKIN AND MARSHALL,
STATIONERS' COURT.

1859.

This Plate represents the same
Face restored to its original &
Youthful appearance by the aid
of Artificial Teeth as supplied by
Mr Howard

PREFACE.

THE want of a concise and familiar Treatise on the Teeth, containing information which may be useful to all those who have lost many of them, suggested the idea of this essay.

There is respecting the Teeth a degree of delicacy generally felt which prevents advice being given even where requisite, and this frequently occurs among intimate friends: in such cases, a recommendation to read this *Treatise* may lead to the most beneficial results.

The author would impress upon all who read, or in any way profit by this work, that it would be *an act of kindness to present it to any friend who may require the aid of a Dentist.*

CONTENTS.

TOOTH-ACHE.

THERE are not any "ills which flesh is heir to" more excruciating or intolerable than, or which so completely incapacitate a person for business or pleasure as, Tooth-ache.

The pain produced by the exposure of the membrane of a tooth to the action of external irritants, is certainly one of the most excruciating to which the human system is liable. The sensation is perfectly *sui generis*, and it is, unfortunately, as unnecessary as it is difficult, to describe it; for few persons who have arrived at adult age, are so happy as to have escaped its attacks. Scarcely tic-douloureux itself is more agonizing for the moment, than a darting paroxysm of tooth-ache. It is not therefore to be wondered at, that every new remedy which professes to cure it, should for a time be eagerly caught at.

The sympathetic affections to which it gives rise are exceedingly various and important; though it is only of late years that they have been properly understood, and the attention of medical men directed to their true source. Now, however, that these remote sympathies have excited a degree of interest more commensurate with their importance; so frequently are they found to occur, that practitioners are, on the other hand, in danger of attributing to this cause, diseases which have not the remotest connexion with it. It not unfrequently happens that parts the most remote become the apparent seat of pain, from the exposure of the nerve of a tooth. I have seen this occur not only in the face, over the scalp, in the ear, or underneath the lower jaw, but down the neck, over the shoulder, and along the whole length of the arm.

It will be readily understood, that irritation in different teeth will be attended by the occurrence of pain referred to, in corresponding situations, more or less remote from its true seat. No one of these is so constant and so distinctly marked, as the violent pain in the ear, produced by the exposed nerve of the inferior *dens sapientiæ*. This is so general an occurrence as to constitute in many cases the only criterion of the true seat of pain, where several contiguous teeth are decayed. Cases of true ear-ache are comparatively rare ; and I am convinced that where no actual *disease* of that origin exist, the pain referred to will be found, very generally, to arise from a decayed inferior *dens sapientiæ ;* and hence, it often happens that blisters behind the ear, and hot applications to that part, produce only a partial and deceptive relief, the pain returning with increased severity, as soon as the mind ceases to be amused by these ineffectual attempts at removing it. *The only true remedy to be relied upon as a permanent cure, is to have the decayed teeth well stopped at an early stage of decay.*

It most frequently happens that the majority of persons who are actively engaged pay little attention to their teeth, until they become painful.

The evils arising from this neglect are too frequently the loss of many, or, in *some cases, all the teeth,* which, by an early visit to the Dentist, might have been preserved.

PRESERVING THE TEETH,
BY
STOPPING OR PLUGGING THEM.

WHEN decay or caries make their appearance in a tooth, HOWEVER SMALL THE APERTURE MAY BE, IT SHOULD BE PLUGGED WITHOUT DELAY. It is a great error to postpone this until the tooth is painful, as the sooner the tooth is stopped the more successful will be the result, and the greater number of years will the tooth or teeth be preserved.

The progress of decay is entirely arrested, and the tooth saved by stopping the hollow with a preparation which excludes the air, and prevents foulness, or the pain and irritation, occasioned by food lodging in it. By the beautiful and useful operation of stopping or plugging teeth, which are greatly injured by caries, they may be preserved for many years, in most instances *during the remainder of life,* and frequently from ten to twenty teeth may be preserved by these means in the same individual.

I will give the following instance of the efficacy of stopping teeth :—" A gentleman who has been my patient since the age of eight, has just paid me a visit ; twenty years have elapsed since I stopped his teeth, yet I found the same old stopping, which I had inserted : *I have no hesitation in affirming this to be one of the most important and useful operations that can be performed."*

The commencement and progress of decay are so insensible, that it may exist many years, and even the person himself often not be aware of it, till it has penetrated the very centre of the tooth ; having reached the cavity, it there commands attention, on account of the severe tooth-ache it occasions.

Of the various operations required for preserving carious teeth, and arresting all further progress of decay, stopping therefore takes the foremost place.

This operation appears to have been among the first undertaken by those persons who assumed the name of Dentist. It was at all times considered to be a *desideratum* among the Profession, to *Discover a White Succedaneum,* which would fill up, permanently, the cavity caused by decay, and *arrest its progress*, and thus preserve the teeth to the latest period of life.

VALUE AND IMPORTANCE OF THE TEETH.*

THE teeth influence the form and expression of the countenance much more than is generally imagined, and the finest face is disfigured if the teeth are irregular, and a disagreeable impression is produced.

Where the teeth are good, there is, when

---

* The importance of the Teeth is such, that they deserve our utmost attention, as well with regard to the preservation of them when in a healthy state, as to the methods of curing them when diseased. They require this attention, not only for the preservation of themselves, as instruments useful to the body, but also on account of other parts with which they are connected; for diseases in the teeth are apt to produce diseases in the neighbouring parts, not unfrequently of serious consequences.— JOHN HUNTER.

He who pays no attention to his teeth, by this single neglect, betrays vulgar sentiments.—LAVATER.

speaking, or smiling especially, a fascination present, which prevents further examination of the countenance.

It is, therefore, evident that much of the beauty of the countenance depends upon a happy and regular disposition of the teeth.

If the countenance of youth is contrasted with that of age, the great difference will be found in the alteration of the mouth.

When the Teeth are lost, the nose and chin approximate, the cheeks become hollow and shrunken, the lips thin and contracted, thus giving an appearance of premature old age.

Good teeth are not only indispensable to *personal beauty*, but on their regularity depends perfect articulation.

The most striking cases are those persons about the middle period of life, who have lost their teeth ; for however clear and perfect their utterance may have been before their loss, it is impossible to regain it without supplying the deficiency by means of artificial teeth.

The most important use of the teeth is mastication of the food, previously to its being received into the stomach. The distressing sensations arising from imperfectly masticated food, must immediately convince every one of the importance of the teeth in the first step towards good digestion, and of the paramount necessity of possessing them, either natural or artificial, as the means of retaining health.

How valuable then are regular and sound teeth, contributing so much beauty and expression even to the finest face.

Can more important or urgent reasons be required to enforce an immediate attention to their preservation ?

Many persons habitually neglect their teeth,

and, from having long seen them discoloured, imagine that they are decayed or corroded beyond all recovery ; this is frequently a mistaken notion, as by a visit to the Dentist that discoloration may be removed without the least injury to the teeth, and they will again appear of their natural colour.

If persons foresaw the consequences of this neglect, they would, no doubt, act differently. A gradual loosening of the teeth is very soon produced by an accumulation of tartar, which almost imperceptibly, although surely, undermines them, and ends in the successive loss of the whole of them.

To preserve the teeth of a fine pearly whiteness, and retain them firm in their sockets, it is necessary to observe strict cleanliness of the mouth, by the use of proper tooth brushes, morning and evening, with tepid water, and occasionally to use tooth powder.

LOOSE TEETH.

THIS is a state of the teeth which prevails to a great extent, and more generally among persons about the middle period of life : especially those who have resided in India, or other warm climates.

Having devoted much time and study to this particular department of dentistry, I have succeeded in applying *a new principle,* for arresting this very prevalent and most destructive state of the gums and teeth ; by which means, teeth that are very loose, and apparently likely to fall out of their sockets, may be rendered firm, and retained for many years.

Even if there be only one or two loose teeth in the mouth, immediate attention should be paid to the case, otherwise they will aggravate the disease by increasing materially the irritation, and consequent inflammation, and thereby most certainly cause the loss of many others.

By resorting to proper means sufficiently early, the teeth and gums may be restored to health.

The principal object is to prevent the extension of the disease, which, if unchecked, will pervade the whole mouth.

CONSIDERATIONS

ON THE HUMAN VOICE,

IN RELATION

TO DENTAL SURGERY.

I DO not intend to enter into a highly scientific consideration of the above subject, but to endeavour to give, as concisely as possible, my experience in relation to it; and to show by what principles we are governed in our practice; seeing that, by former methods, and the practice of too great a number at the present time, much inconvenience is experienced by a disregard to a proper consideration of the organs of speech, in operations generally upon the teeth.

It would seem that few have any idea of the *physiology* of the voice, and still less have

B

they *thought* upon the subject. That we have had great satisfaction by considering well the nature of the defects in the speech, in operating upon the teeth, and especially in setting artificial teeth, is true ; while in the absence of such consideration much mischief would have resulted. If I can, therefore, succeed in directing the attention of some of the public to this subject, my labours will be rewarded.

That the dental organs are largely concerned in enunciation, all will, I doubt not, allow. What are the first lispings of childhood, but the effects of the imperfect development of the organs of speech, of which the teeth, gums, and alveoli form an important part? Mark their changes from their earliest manifestations, modified by every change to mature development of the system generally, as well as by the organs of speech, up to the full, clear, and robust development of adult life.

The Larynx is the principal organ concerned in effecting or producing what is called the voice. But many organs are necessarily concerned along with it. The *trachea*, the *lungs, diaphragm*, and *abdominal muscles*, below it: the *glottis, velum-palati, nares, roof of the mouth, gums, teeth, lips,* and *tongue,* above or outside of the larynx. No voice can be perfect with either of these organs imperfect, or in an abnormal condition. And it is well for the dentist, when he discovers that he cannot produce an agreeable voice in setting teeth for a patient, whom he had not known previously to his loss of them, to consider whether any defect complained of depended upon a mal-arrangement of his own work, or whether nature, or the health and habits of the patient, were at fault. The dentist ought to be sufficiently familiar with all the organs of speech and their peculiar functions, to judge which one, or more, is or are not properly performing their respective functions; whether difficulties complained of, depend upon a loss of any or all of the teeth, their mal-arrangement or disease, the imperfect development of the alveolar processes, and what sounds are most affected by the loss of either or all of the teeth. As, for instance, a loss of the posterior teeth is calculated to affect some sounds more than others. A loss of the front teeth, superior or inferior, affects different sounds differently ; hence a correct idea of the *"articulations,"* or articulate sounds, of the organs of speech is necessary. For instance, we must know whether it be a *labial,* a *dento-lingual,* or *guttural* sound that is defective, before a remedy can be applied ; and precisely in what way it is deranged and requires to be modified.

What we mean by the *"articulations,"* is the manner in which the column of air is stopped or restrained by the approximation or contact of the walls or sides of the vocal tube, as the air is impelled through it by the lungs, diaphragm, &c., in effecting enunciation. For instance, the lips must be brought in contact with each other, and then separated suddenly to pronounce the letters B and P. These are labial articulations. The margins of the tongue must be placed in close contact with the gums and necks of the teeth of the superior jaw, and dwell there for an instant, in the same manner as the lips are brought in contact to stop the column of air in the labial sounds, then suddenly removed, to effect the sounds of the letters T and D. And the root of the tongue and veil of the palate must be brought in contact in like manner, to pronounce the letters K and Q.

Very frequently great defect is produced by a loss of the back teeth, and especially when great absorption of the gums and alveoli take place, simply because the tongue cannot close the tube laterally, but allows the air to escape into the cheeks, producing a very defective enunciation. Similar effects are produced in articulating *te, ne, re,* and *le.*

I corrected a marked defect of this nature in the case of a Gentleman, in 1843, by setting teeth behind the canines, three on one side and two on the other, by simply joining the stay plates together, and forming an even surface with the other teeth. In this way, the margins of the tongue could form an air-tight joint, so to speak, along its lateral margins, which prevented completely the escape of the air into the cheeks. He was considered by his friends a regular stammerer; in fact, in speaking, his cheeks were vibrating like a pair of bellows.

Again, it will be observed, that, as the air rushes over the apex of the tongue, the sounds will be modified by the front incisors being very close together or very far apart; hence, in filing teeth, very marked changes are sometimes produced in the voice; also by the loss of a single tooth. If the tongue cannot come forward on account of the extreme narrowness of the upper jaw and projecting position of the front teeth, there will be lisping on this sound and on the articulation of *te*.

Now it is clear that if any of the teeth are destroyed, and the margins of the gums rendered very uneven, so that the tongue cannot accommodate itself properly to the margins, all the words in which this articulation occurs will be proportionately defective; hence in setting artificial teeth, either partial, or full sets, if care is not taken to restore the natural relations of the mouth generally, and especially the principal relations which are broken, but little good will be effected, and most commonly mischief will be done.*

---

* Wolfgang Kemplin, who invented that very ingenious deception, the Automaton Chess-Player, which seems for a time to have puzzled all the philosophers and mathematicians of Europe, constructed a speaking automaton, in which he ultimately succeeded so far as to make it pronounce several sentences, among the best of which were —"Romanorum imperator semper Augustus;" "Leopoldus secundus;" "Vous êtes mon ami;" "Je vous aime de tout mon cœur." It was some years, however, before he could accomplish more than the simple utterance of the

PRESERVATION OF THE TEETH BY MECHANICAL MEANS.

As long as the appearances are preserved by the presence of the front teeth, the loss of the side teeth, or grinders, is frequently viewed as a matter of little importance. This is a great error, for it is the presence of the grinders which keeps the mouth sufficiently open to prevent the front teeth from coming

---

sounds o, ou, and e. Year after year, we are told, was devoted to this machine, but i or u, or any of the consonants, refused to obey his summons. At length, he added, at the open extremity of the vocal tube, an apparatus, similar in action and construction to the *human mouth*, WITH ITS TEETH, when he quickly succeeded in making it not only pronounce the consonants, but words, and even the sentences quoted above. He had previously imitated the tongue, and its actions. This fact is interesting, not only as a rare instance of human ingenuity, (for, if not the first, it was probably the most perfect instrument of the kind that had then been constructed,) but also as exhibiting in a most striking light, the beautiful adaptation of parts to their respective functions; and that so perfect are the contrivances in Nature for particular ends, that, in order to arrive at anything like an imitation of those functions, we must follow closely the method she employs.

in contact during mastication. When, therefore, the grinders are lost, and their places are not supplied by artificial means, the front teeth soon become either worn away, or loosened and pushed from their sockets.

Few persons are aware of the cause of losing their front teeth. Some attribute the loss to a local defect in the teeth themselves, and others to constitutional causes. They seldom or never reflect that the front teeth were not intended, and hence, are not adapted, for masticating purposes, which invariably destroy them. The entire process of mastication belongs to the grinders, and the only function which the front teeth are intended to perform is comprised in the word " cutting," which their name *incisors* implies.

When even a single grinder is lost, the whole of the teeth on that side of the jaw are weakened by the breach which it leaves, and which deprives them of mutual lateral support, and renders them apt to be pushed from their proper perpendicular position, towards the opening, by the opposite teeth. But this is not all; for as soon as a tooth in one jaw loses its masticating opponent in the other, it begins to protrude from its socket, loosen, and ultimately fall out. So that the loss of one tooth, by rendering its opponent in the other jaw useless, amounts to the loss of two.

When the teeth remaining for mastication are too few in number to sustain the force of the jaws, they are soon destroyed, by being either forced into their sockets, so as to produce disease and absorption, or crushed and broken, occasioning grievous pain, followed by the total loss of such teeth. The front teeth, being unprotected, through the loss of the grinders, are soon destroyed in the way before described; and proper mastication being now impossible, derangement of the digestive function ensues, attended by privation of comfort and loss of health.

Fortunately, the whole of this mischief may be remedied, and the greater part of it prevented, by the timely adoption of artificial teeth. When any of the side teeth are lost, their places should be immediately supplied by properly constructed artificial teeth, so as to prevent the others from slanting towards the opening left by those which are lost. Artificial teeth, by meeting the natural teeth in the opposite jaw, preserve them by preventing their protrusion from their sockets ; and mastication being thus restored, health is recovered and preserved. *The artificial teeth, by preventing the jaws from shutting too close, preserve the front teeth, which would otherwise be destroyed, by meeting together in the process of mastication.*

The object in supplying artificial teeth has, hitherto, been too generally confined to mere show, at the expense of the other teeth; whereas, the whole aim should be to preserve the remaining teeth, and restore mastication,

which secures comfort and health. When
many teeth are lost, all tampering with the
remainder can only increase suffering, and
hasten the loss of teeth so tampered with.
The operator must be perfectly aware of
this; but as the continual suffering produces
constant visits, and unmerited fees, to the
operator, those unhappy patients are the
most profitable to him. Such practitioners,
instead of pointing out the proper artist
capable of affording the only real relief,
strenuously advise their patient dupes *against*
the adoption of preservative pieces of artificial
teeth; for mere operators, being incapable of
supplying this remedy themselves, know that
delusion would be dispelled, and their mal-
practices exposed, if their victims fell into the
hands of a competent mechanical artist.

The art of supplying lost teeth so as satis-
factorily to answer all the purposes of natural
ones, and at the same time not only without
doing injury, but to give support to, and

preserve those that remain, was very imperfectly understood until late years.

The very great perfection which this art has now attained, would scarcely be believed by those who are not familiar with the subject.

ARTIFICIAL TEETH.

PHILOSOPHICAL PRINCIPLES ON WHICH ARTIFICIAL TEETH ARE FORMED.

To give entire ease and comfort to the wearer, the artist must be capable of engraving his work to fit the gums so perfectly *air-tight*, that it shall adhere and remain securely firm in its place for the purposes of mastication, &c., by the mere force of *capillary attraction*, and the *pressure of the atmosphere.*

The principles have been frequently described, yet few people give credence to them as applied to artificial teeth, although nothing is more just, correct, and natural. The common water-pump acts on the latter principle, and there is no other on which artificial teeth can be constructed that will not soon destroy the remaining teeth.

In the introduction of anything new in science, there is wanting a corresponding language by which it may be expressed, in order that it may be described on paper so as to be understood by the reader. Capillary attraction, and atmospheric pressure, may be thus explained :—

Capillary attraction is the principle by which a fluid is strongly attracted between closely fitting surfaces, and the closer the surfaces approach each other, the more strongly do they attract the fluid, which thus expels and excludes the air. It is by capillary attraction that water rises into and fills a sponge.

Atmospheric pressure, which was formerly explained by means of the axiom, that *nature abhors a vacuum,* is owing to the weight of the atmosphere, which causes it to bear on all bodies, near the surface of the earth, with a pressure of about fourteen pounds on each square inch.

On my principle of supplying a deficiency of teeth, the artificial piece being fitted close to the gum, the natural moisture of the mouth is affected by capillary attraction, the moment the piece is introduced into its place; and the moisture being drawn in between the piece and the gum, the intervening air is driven out, and being thus excluded, the atmosphere acts with a force in proportion to the extent of the surfaces in contact, in keeping the artificial piece in its place. The force, even on a small piece, is considerable, and on large pieces frequently exceeds thirty pounds; yet even in these cases the wearer feels no pressure beyond secure adhesion. *The piece itself seldom weighs above half an ounce,* and is easily removed, at the pleasure of the wearer, by merely raising one of its extremities with the tongue.

One of the most *familiar instances of the joint effects of capillary attraction* and *atmospheric pressure,* is perhaps that *exhibited by the schoolboy with what is called the sucker.* This toy consists of a string passed through the centre of a piece of thick leather soaked in water, which, being pressed on a large stone, adheres to it so firmly that the stone may be lifted up and carried away by it.

Pieces of teeth made of the tusk of hippopotamus feel in every way congenial to the mouth, and cannot be distinguished by the tongue from the natural gum and teeth; and being fitted in the manner just described, adhering to the *gum only,* afford support to the remaining teeth, which are let into grooves accurately formed in the piece for their reception. This prevents tooth-ache, and other painful sensations, by shielding tender teeth and stumps from change of temperature and extraneous matters. The jarring of the *front teeth* on each other is obviated by the piece preventing the mouth from shutting too close. Mastication and articulation are restored, and the premature appearance of age and deformity completely removed. When a few weeks have familiarized the wearer to the change, he becomes almost unconscious that he uses artificial teeth ; and as cheerful spirits return with health and comfortable feeling, happiness, " the end and aim of our existence," is restored, and life prolonged and enjoyed, perhaps, ten or twenty years beyond the period to which it would other wise be limited.

IT IS THE DUTY OF ALL, AND THE WISH OF THE BENEVOLENT, TO PRESERVE THEIR HEALTH AND PERSONAL APPEARANCE FOR THE SATISFACTION OF THOSE WHO LOVE THEM.

C

Either partial or entire sets of teeth, scientifically designed, and skilfully adapted, may be worn with the greatest ease and satisfaction; but, on the contrary, those that are ill made and unskilfully adapted, are troublesome to the wearer, an impediment to speech and mastication, and even a greater blemish to the countenance than the want of teeth; those *that are well adapted, are, on the contrary, easy, useful, and highly ornamental.*

In the construction of artificial teeth, utility and comfort, as much as appearance, ought to be considered by the Dentist. The latter refers to the successful imitation of nature, in the form, colour, and proportions of the teeth, and especially in the shape and expression of the mouth.*

---

* In consequence of the complete or even partial ruin of the teeth, the face shrinks, the voice loses its harmony, becomes shrill, or is lowered, and the pronunciation, of course, very imperfect. The countenance assumes a different expression, is harsh or morose, the flesh of the cheeks

THE ATTENTION OF THOSE WHO REQUIRE ARTIFICIAL TEETH, IS ESPECIALLY DIRECTED TO THE FOLLOWING OBSERVATIONS :—

The *extraction* of the few teeth or roots which may remain in the mouth is insisted upon by many Dentists, previously to taking a model of the mouth, for the purpose of preparing artificial teeth.

This is *never necessary*, as, by the author's improved method of supplying the loss of teeth, from one to a complete set can be fitted in the mouth, with the greatest accuracy and precision, answering most fully every purpose of articulation and mastication ; and so perfectly natural in appearance as to defy detection by the closest observer,

---

will flag and hang down, and *wrinkles will prematurely furrow the face.*

The mouth and nose also change ; the chin seems to be longer; in short, every part of the face is discomposed, in a more or less offensive degree, and presents the sight of painful destruction.—JERBAUX.

C 2

without extracting any teeth or stumps, or giving any pain. He, therefore, would strongly urge those who require artificial teeth *never* to submit to have any tooth or stump extracted for that purpose, as if only one tooth remain, or even stumps, they are of essential service in assisting to keep the artificial teeth steady in the mouth, and are of great advantage in many other respects—therefore, they *should never be extracted.**

Whenever a partial loss of the double teeth has occurred, painful or uneasy sensations are experienced in the front teeth; these are warnings of the destruction about to ensue.

---

* As some persons are under an apprehension that they must be put to great pain and inconvenience by the removal of teeth and stumps, and other painful operations, before they can be supplied with artificial teeth, I feel it incumbent on me to remove this error, so far as it relates to my system, which requires no removal of teeth or stumps, or any pain or inconvenience whatever, any more than if the article in question were an ordinary piece of dress.

The front teeth separate, afterwards take irregular positions, projecting outwards, or inclining inwards, and soon become loose.

By filling up the spaces left by the lost double teeth with artificial ones, and lengthening the grinding surfaces of those remaining in the mouth, such defects are obviated.

To effect this, much labour and skill are required, but, when accomplished, it restores the mouth to a state equal to the natural one, and renders the patient easy and comfortable

Here are two objects to be obtained:

First.—To supply the artificial teeth where every second or third natural one has been extracted, and those that remain are decayed or worn to stumps.

Second.—To lengthen the grinding surface of the remaining back teeth, and thus render those decayed teeth or stumps of essential service in supporting and steadying artificial ones.

Ligatures should not be used to fasten artificial teeth ; they should be so constructed as to be removed as easily as a glove, and yet be perfectly secure and steady in the mouth ; objects which can only be attained by a Dentist who perfectly understands his profession.

In all cases, by very great accuracy of fitting on the model, and a correct adaptation to the mouth, fastenings with clasps or ligatures are rendered unnecessary.

In cases where there is absorption or loss of substance, a very great change takes place in the appearance and expression of the countenance. It is not the fact that the change in the form of the lower jaw is the result of old age, for it is rather the inevitable result of the total loss of the teeth. Thus old persons having preserved them, have the angle of the jaw nearly acute, and the chin scarcely projecting ; whilst we meet with many adults who have lost all their teeth at an EARLY AGE, and who have nevertheless the entire physiognomy of OLD AGE.—*See the Engraving.*

This absorption occurs more or less in all cases ; and to ascertain the extent of such loss of substance is very important previously to supplying artificial teeth ; as, by a judicious arrangement of the material, in making good such losses with artificial gum as well as teeth, where the loss is considerable, depends that perfect restoration of the features to their natural symmetry, which the art of Dentistry is capable of giving.

By attention to the above, any degree of fulness of the lips or cheeks can be obtained, without inconvenience to the wearer.

Much has been said with respect to the comparative merits of bone or gold as the frame for artificial teeth ; some Dentists using bone in every case, however inapplicable ; others using gold, although perhaps equally so, in that particular case.

An *invariable adherence* to either plan, deprives the person seeking assistance of those comforts and great advantages which the art of a skilful Dentist is capable of affording.

Ivory, or the tusk of the Hippopotamus, soon decomposes, and, notwithstanding the greatest care and cleanliness, will not last long.

It is in all cases desirable to place as *little in the mouth as possible*, that the articulation and mastication may be performed with more freedom.

Gold of the finest quality can be used with the greatest advantage, as it may be thin and small in size, and yet possess infinitely more durability than Ivory, which, when made thin, is very soon destroyed, and therefore, from the necessity of frequently renewing it, becomes expensive.

The teeth that are usually supplied by Dentists, are either natural or mineral.

Natural teeth have been long employed by the most celebrated Dentists, and with great success as regards appearance and utility; but with respect to their durability, the time they will last varies according to the constitution of the wearer, notwithstanding their handsome appearance when first placed in the mouth.

Some persons of extreme sensibility and delicacy of feeling, will not wear natural teeth under any circumstances; although there is not any rational objection to their use, as there is not any real difference between them and ivory.

Many persons, however, do object to wear them; and their being liable to decompose and become discoloured in so short a time, induced me to bestow much time and study to find a substitute which should combine an equally natural appearance and utility, with *much greater durability*.

This most desirable object is now attained, by my having invented a *new description of Composition Teeth*, composed of siliceous substances, with a very fine enamel upon them, which admits of every variety of shade and colour, and enables me to match, with the greatest nicety, both in *form* and *colour*, any teeth that may remain in the mouth.

They are perfectly *Incorrodible*, and cannot be affected in any way by the saliva, heat of the stomach, or acids of any kind ; IN SHORT, THEIR DURABILITY IS UNBOUNDED, AS THEY WILL NEVER DECAY OR BECOME THE LEAST DISCOLOURED, AND WILL APPEAR AS WELL

AFTER TEN YEARS' WEAR AS THEY DID THE FIRST DAY THEY WERE PLACED IN THE MOUTH.

So closely do they resemble Nature, that many have been deceived, supposing them to be natural teeth.

The Author will be happy to show them in every variety to those who are interested in this subject; WHEN THIS STATEMENT OF THEIR SUPERIORITY OVER ALL OTHERS WILL BE FOUND TO BE ENTIRELY AND SCRUPULOUSLY CORRECT.

THE CHEMICAL COMPOSITION OF THE TEETH.

THE analytical processes to which several celebrated chemists have submitted the teeth, have afforded results differing in some trifling circumstances from each other. It is a matter of very little practical importance whether the proportion of phosphate of lime to animal matter, or that of carbonate of lime to either, be one or two per cent. greater or less; but, as a point of accuracy merely, it may perhaps be desirable that our account should be as nearly correct as possible.

The following is the result given by Berzelius, whose analysis appears to have been more elaborate than that of any other chemist. It will be found to record the occurrence of several substances as existing in the enamel and bone of the teeth, the presence of which has not been detected by others. According to this celebrated chemist, the enamel of the adult teeth contains in 100 parts,—

Phosphate of lime	85·3
Fluate of lime	3·2
Carbonate of lime	8·
Phosphate of magnesia	1·5
Soda and muriate of soda	1·
Animal matter and water	1·
	100·

The bony substance is stated, by the same authority, to contain,—

Phosphate of lime	62·
Fluate of lime	2·
Carbonate of lime	5·5
Phosphate of magnesia	1·
Soda and muriate of soda	⟩ 1·5
Gelatine and water	28·
	100·

The following is a tabular view of the results obtained by Mr. Pepys :—

	Bone of Tempy. Teeth.	Bone of Adult Teeth.	Roots of Adult Teeth.	Enamel.
Phosphate of lime . .	62	64	58	78
Carbonate of lime . .	6	6	4	6
Cartilage	20	20	28	0
Water and loss . . .	12	10	10	16
	100	100	100	100

PHYSIOLOGICAL OBSERVATIONS

ON THE

NATURAL FOOD OF MAN,

DEDUCED FROM THE CHARACTERS OF THE TEETH.

———

FROM the foregoing view of the nature and offices of the different classes of the teeth, it appears that their structure and uses are more perfectly equalised in the human subject than in any other animal. It is true that, in some tribes of animals, whose habits require the greatest possible extension of the office of a particular class of teeth, a corresponding development of that class is found to take place, to a much greater degree than in man. Thus, in the *carnivora*, the cuspidati are greatly elongated and strengthened, in order to enable them to seize their food, and to tear it in pieces; in the *rodentia*, or gnawing

animals, as in the beaver for instance, the
incisors are remarkably long, and exhibit that
extraordinary development which their peculiar habits demand; and, in the gramini-
vorous animals, the *ruminantia* especially,
the molares are found to occupy the most
conspicuous situation. But, in each of these
instances, the other kinds of teeth are found
to be proportionally of less importance, and
in some cases are actually wanting. In man,
on the contrary, every class appears to be
equally developed, to a moderate, though a
sufficient, degree, and to exhibit a perfection
of structure, which may be considered as
the true type, from which all other forms
are mere deviations. It becomes, therefore,
a question of some interest, and perhaps of
no less difficulty, to what food the structure
which has just been demonstrated is particularly adapted. The opinion which I
venture to give has not been hastily formed,
nor without what appeared to me sufficient
grounds; I advance it, however, with dif-

fidence, and do not profess to consider it as much more than hypothetical.

The endowment of reason, that greatest, best gift of the Creator, appears, if we consider the perfection of human organization, to be particularly, and, in its highest degree, even exclusively, adapted to the conformation and requirements of man. This high and divine endowment should never be lost sight of in our reasonings on the human structure, and the physiology and habits of our species; as it is only with the allowances and modifications, which the possession of a quality so infinitely higher than the instinct of other animals necessarily supposes, that the actual habits of man can be viewed as compatible with his organization. Although these habits, — now essentially arising from, and combined with, a state of civilization, which, in a greater or less degree, must be allowed to exist in every known tribe of our species, — cannot be considered, in any one instance, as actually and exclusively *natural;* yet we may be led, by a careful examination of the structure of the different organs, and by an analogical comparison of them as they exist in man, with the same organs in those animals which most nearly resemble him in structure, but which are still found in a perfectly natural state, to a plausible supposition, at least, of what were originally his natural habits; and which would have still continued so, but for those changes which have arisen from the possession of this very endowment.

With this view of the subject, it is not, I think, going too far to say that every fact connected with the human organization goes to prove, that man was originally formed a frugivorous animal, and, therefore, probably tropical, or nearly so, with regard to his geographical situation. This opinion is principally derived from the formation of

D

his teeth and digestive organs, as well as from the character of his skin, and the general structure of his limbs. It is not my intention now to go further into the discussion of this subject, than to observe, that, if analogy be allowed to have any weight in the argument, it is wholly on that side of the question which I have just taken. Those animals, whose teeth and digestive apparatus most nearly resemble our own, namely, the apes and monkeys, are undoubtedly frugivorous; but as, from their organization, they are necessarily tropical animals, and without the gift of reason, by which they might have overcome the difference of temperature by artificial means, they remain still restricted to their original food, and confined to the very limited climate to which their structure peculiarly adapted them. The reasoning powers of man, on the contrary, have enabled him to set climate at defiance, and have rendered him, in all cases, more or less an artificial being. No longer restrained within that range of temperature to which the delicacy of his frame, no less than the nature of his original nutriment, would have confined him, he becomes the denizen of every climate, and the lord of terrestrial creation.

DISEASES OF THE TEETH.

OF THE PREDISPOSING AND REMOTE CAUSES OF DENTAL CARIES.

BY predisposing or constitutional causes, I mean those which are inherent in the original structure and constitution of the teeth, whether hereditary, or induced by circumstances operating during their formation; and by remote causes, I intend those which, by producing *subsequent* changes in their condition, render them more liable to be acted upon by any of the *exciting* causes of the disease.

Hereditary predisposition is amongst the most common and remarkable of the former class. It often happens that this tendency exists in either the whole, or great part of a family of children, where one of the parents had been similarly affected; and this is true to so great an extent, that I have very commonly seen the same tooth, and even the same part of the tooth, affected in several individuals of the family, and at about the same age. In other instances, where there are many children, amongst whom there exists a distinct division into two portions, some resembling the father, and others the mother, in features and constitution, I have observed a corresponding difference in the teeth, both as it regards their form and texture, and their tendency to decay.

The whole list of infantile diseases, operating during the formation of the permanent teeth, are to be considered as so many causes predisposing to caries: as the irritation excited by the first dentition for instance, and all the various morbid actions consequent upon it. Not the diseases alone of this period, but some of the remedies also which are em-

ployed for their cure, exert a most injurious
influence upon the future constitution of the
teeth. *The immoderate use of mercury in
early infancy, produces more, perhaps, than
any other similar cause, that universal tendency to decay, which, in many instances,
destroys almost every tooth at an early age.*
It is certainly not unimportant to bear this
fact in mind, in the administration of this
"sovereign remedy," this panacea, as many
appear to consider it, in infantile diseases.

A strumous constitution is very often ac-
companied by early and general decay of the
teeth. I will instance one case, which, however, possesses no claim of peculiarity for its
selection. It but too much resembles many
others that every practitioner must be ac-
quainted with.

"A young lady, seventeen years of age,
possessing that remarkable transparency of
skin, and delicacy of features, which too

often indicate incipient consumption, con-
sulted me respecting the state of her teeth.
The enamel, where it remained, was of that
beautiful pearly whiteness and transparency
which characterize teeth of a weak and
frail texture; but there was not a single
tooth, either in the upper or lower jaw,
which was not to a greater or less degree
the subject of caries. Not one even of the
inferior incisors, so seldom attacked by
disease, had escaped its ravages."

That morbid affections of the constitution
occurring during the formation of the teeth,
produce in them a predisposition to decay,
receives a strong confirmation from the fact
that in the greater number of cases they become diseased in pairs; for in whatever
changes the constitution may suffer at that
period, the teeth, then in the progress of their
formation, would naturally participate, and
would be rendered more or less liable to
disease, in proportion to the injury thus in-

flicted on them. Upon the period, therefore, at which these constitutional disorders take place, it will, to a certain degree, depend which teeth shall be most predisposed to decay.

Amongst the *remote* causes, or those which produce a deleterious *change* in the constitution of the teeth subsequent to their formation, one of the most extensive in its effects is the use of mercury.

To the profuse administration of this remedy in tropical diseases, we may, I think, in a great measure, attribute the injury which a residence in hot climates so frequently inflicts on the teeth. It must not, however, be considered as the exclusive, or even the principal source of this evil; for fevers of every kind, dyspepsia, and, in short, every severe or long-continued constitutional disorder, must be classed amongst the most remote causes of dental caries.

OF THE EXCITING CAUSES OF
DENTAL CARIES.

FROM the view which has been taken of the nature and proximate cause of this disease, it is evident, that whatever has a tendency to produce inflammation in the teeth, may become an exciting cause of it; probably the most frequent of these is any sudden or considerable change of temperature, whether the effect of exposure to a cold atmosphere, or of taking very hot or very cold substances into the mouth. As a general rule it may be observed, that whatever is placed in contact with the teeth, either so much higher or lower than the natural temperature of the body, as to produce pain, may probably prove to be the exciting cause of the disease; thus drinking very hot fluids on one hand, and, on the other, taking ice, without the precaution of preventing it lying in contact with the teeth, are, I am convinced, fertile sources of disease in these organs. When the extremely dense,

solid structure of the teeth is considered, it
will not appear wonderful that this result
should occur from change of temperature in
a part, the unyielding nature of which pre-
cludes the possibility of expansion and con-
traction, not only in the vessels of its substance, but also in the membrane filling its
cavity.

The teeth most liable to mortification are,
undoubtedly, the dentes sapientiæ; and I
have even known many instances in which,
when they first made their appearance through
the gum, they were already in a state of partial
decay. This probably arises from their being
formed at a later period of life than the other
teeth, when the constitution is doubtless in
a less favourable state for the production of
newly formed parts than during early infancy,
when the process of new formation is going on
with rapidity in every part of the system.
The first molares are also frequently decayed
at an early age; so much so, that it is often

necessary to remove these teeth, in consequence of severe suffering from tooth-ache, even before many others of the permanent set are perfected. The cuspidati, both superior and inferior, are comparatively seldom the subjects of disease; and the inferior incisors still more rarely.

Every part of the crown appears to be equally liable to caries. In the molares it attacks alike the centre of the masticating surface, the side in contact with the next tooth, and the outer and inner surfaces; the incisors are often carious at the point of contact, and now and then the superior lateral incisors become first decayed at the centre of the posterior surfaces.

It is generally supposed that there are two distinct kinds of dental caries, as it assumes very different appearances in different individuals; being sometimes quite white, at others brown or blackish. These varieties, however, for they are nothing more, depend upon the constitution of the teeth, and the circumstances under which decay has commenced. If the teeth were originally of a delicate texture, formed under a weakly or scrofulous state of the constitution, the progress of the caries is generally very rapid, and the decayed part becomes soft and of a whitish colour; but if they possess a more dense and firm structure, and were formed in a healthy state of the system, the decay, when it does occur, is much more tardy in its advance, and the affected portion is always of a dark brown or blackish hue. The cause of this difference appears to be, that, in the former case, its progress is so rapid that the decomposition is imperfect, and no change of colour therefore takes place;—in the latter, its advance is so slow as to allow of a more complete decomposition, and the decaying substance consequently becomes more or less darkened.

Whatever tends to irritate and inflame the

gum, must in a greater or less degree produce a corresponding irritation in the teeth, from the close connexion which subsists between them ; and hence the accumulation of tartar, portions of food remaining between the teeth, or any similar circumstance, may possibly become an exciting cause of caries ; and this, not only by means of inflammation propagated through the gum, but also by the exposure of the necks of the teeth to external agents, in consequence of the absorption of the gum and alveolar processes. The necessity of keeping the teeth in a constant state of cleanliness, and freedom from all extraneous substances, is therefore enjoined as one of the best means of preventing the occurrence of caries from the causes just mentioned.